Dear Parent:

Congratulations! Your child is taking the first steps on an exciting journey. The destination? Independent reading!

STEP INTO READING® will help your child get there. The program offers five steps to reading success. Each step includes fun stories and colorful art. There are also Step into Reading Sticker Books, Step into Reading Math Readers, Step into Reading Phonics Readers, Step into Reading Write-In Readers, and Step into Reading Phonics Boxed Sets—a complete literacy program with something for every child.

Learning to Read, Step by Step!

Ready to Read   Preschool–Kindergarten
• big type and easy words • rhyme and rhythm • picture clues
For children who know the alphabet and are eager to begin reading.

Reading with Help   Preschool–Grade 1
• basic vocabulary • short sentences • simple stories
For children who recognize familiar words and sound out new words with help.

Reading on Your Own   Grades 1–3
• engaging characters • easy-to-follow plots • popular topics
For children who are ready to read on their own.

Reading Paragraphs   Grades 2–3
• challenging vocabulary • short paragraphs • exciting stories
For newly independent readers who read simple sentences with confidence.

Ready for Chapters   Grades 2–4
• chapters • longer paragraphs • full-color art
For children who want to take the plunge into chapter books but still like colorful pictures.

STEP INTO READING® is designed to give every child a successful reading experience. The grade levels are only guides. Children can progress through the steps at their own speed, developing confidence in their reading, no matter what their grade.

Remember, a lifetime love of reading starts with a single step!

Copyright © 2012 Disney/Pixar. All rights reserved. Published in the United States by Random House Children's Books, a division of Random House, Inc., 1745 Broadway, New York, NY 10019, and in Canada by Random House of Canada Limited, Toronto, in conjunction with Disney Enterprises, Inc. This work was originally published in different form as *Boo on the Loose* by Random House Children's Books in 2002.

Step into Reading, Random House, and the Random House colophon are registered trademarks of Random House, Inc.

Visit us on the Web!
StepIntoReading.com
randomhouse.com/kids

Educators and librarians, for a variety of teaching tools, visit us at RHTeachersLibrarians.com

ISBN: 978-0-7364-2860-6 (trade) – ISBN: 978-0-7364-8103-8 (lib. bdg.)

Printed in the United States of America
10 9 8 7 6

DISNEY·PIXAR
MONSTERS, INC.
Boo on the Loose

By Gail Herman

Illustrated by Scott Tilley,
Floyd Norman, and Brooks Campbell

Random House 🏠 New York

Sulley worked
at Monsters, Inc.
His job
was scaring children.

Monsters went through
bedroom doors
to scare kids.

The whole city ran

on energy from screams!

Late one night,
Sulley saw a door
on the Scare Floor.

Sulley was confused.
He opened the door
and peeked inside.

It was a girl's bedroom.
The girl entered
the monster world!
Her name was Boo.

Sulley was afraid
of Boo.
Children were toxic
to monsters!

Sulley took Boo
to his friend Mike.
Mike was not happy.
Boo scared him, too.

Mike had a plan.
They would leave
Boo in the park.

They went to the park.

Boo stayed in the car.

She locked the doors.

Mike and Sulley
could not get in!

Then Boo saw
a butterfly.
She got out
of the car.

The butterfly flew
into the woods.
Boo chased it.

Mike and Sulley
had lost Boo!
Mike wanted to leave.

But Sulley did not want
to follow the plan.
Sulley liked Boo.

Mike went to the car.

It would not start!

FULL

EMPTY

Sulley had a new plan.

Boo's scream

would start the car!

Sulley ran
into the woods.
He would find Boo.

Boo was happy

to see Sulley.

Boo gave Sulley
a big hug.
They were friends.

Sulley and Boo
found Mike.
He was waiting
in the car.

Sulley smiled.

Boo did not

scare him now.

Sulley and Boo
got back in the car.
They still needed
Boo's scream.

But Boo was smiling.
Sulley did not want
to scare her.

Mike was mad.

He bumped his head

on the steering wheel.

The horn went <u>honk</u>!

Boo laughed.
Her laugh
started the car!

Mike was happy.

Sulley was happy.

Boo was happy.

It was time to go home.